The Secret Life of
HAROLD THE BIRD WATCHER

Weekly Reader Books presents

The Secret Life of

HAROLD THE BIRD WATCHER

Hila Colman

illustrated by Charles Robinson

THOMAS Y. CROWELL COMPANY   NEW YORK

This book is a presentation of
Weekly Reader Books.
Weekly Reader Books offers
book clubs for children from
preschool to young adulthood. All
quality hardcover books are selected
by a distinguished Weekly Reader
Selection Board.

For further information write to:
Weekly Reader Books
1250 Fairwood Ave.
Columbus, Ohio 43216

LIBRARY OF CONGRESS CATALOGING IN PUBLICATION DATA
Colman, Hila.
The secret life of Harold the bird watcher.
SUMMARY: A nine-year-old loner discovers through
an act of heroism that being true to oneself is in itself heroic.
[1. Conduct of life—Fiction] I. Robinson, Charles.
II. Title.   PZ7.C67715Se   [Fic]   77-17075
ISBN 0-690-01306-X   ISBN 0-690-03830-5 lib. bdg.

*This book
is for Jacquie*

Harold always woke up fast. As soon as he opened his eyes he jumped out of bed. On this particular bright, sunny June morning, Harold flung off his light blanket and grabbed the stick he had put beside his bed the night before. But Harold had not slept in his snug little upstairs bedroom with the dormer windows—not Harold. He had cuddled deep in the moss of a green forest and the stick had been a spear to protect him from huge anteaters. (He had seen pictures of them in a book at school.) His mother didn't know it, but Harold had slept in his underwear. Who would wear pajamas in the middle of a forest? A loincloth made more sense.

"Hi, Jumper, come here, Jumper, we've got to be off." Harold called his white stallion, and with spear in hand, he was up and heading through the forest. Nimbly, he slid off his horse and crouched in the bushes, the anteaters of the night before gone. Today he was stalking a strange, fierce, forest monster. . . .

"Harold, Harold," his mother called. "Come down for breakfast, you'll be late for school."

"Okay, okay."

In a jiffy Harold pulled on his jeans and a shirt and joined his mother in the kitchen. Harold gulped down his juice quickly. His father had already left on his milk route, and Harold's mother would soon be off for her job at the hospital. Many times his mother wasn't home when he got back from school because she often worked the afternoon-evening shift, and his father was only there sometimes. When he had finished his milk route, his father did odd jobs in the afternoon. Harold told them he wasn't afraid to be alone, but he felt that they thought he was peculiar not to be. Once his teacher had asked his mother to come to school because she thought he was too shy and that a nine-year-old shouldn't spend so much time alone.

After that, for a while, his mother had nagged him to invite friends home after school, or to go to other children's houses, but Harold had done neither. He guessed he was peculiar. Once he had had a friend, but the friend had moved away and somehow he had never made another. Maybe because he lived outside of the village, or because his parents kept to themselves and didn't socialize either—Harold didn't know why, but the rare times he had been invited to a party, and had gone, he didn't have much fun and felt out of it. Sometimes his mother would look at him with unhappy eyes and say, "Oh, dear, I wish you weren't such a loner. You've got to make an effort."

Harold had nothing to say when she spoke to him like that. But he felt terrible. He felt he was a big disappointment to his parents, and he didn't know how to remedy the situation. He didn't know how to make friends, and his parents didn't know how to show him. His father said, "Your mother and I work hard all day and when we come home we're ready to go to bed early. We don't have time for friends, but you don't have to be that way. We would have liked to have more children, but your mother couldn't have any more—we worry about you, being alone so much."

On his way to school that morning, Harold pretended he was someone like Robin Hood, a gallant robber who took from the rich to help the poor. He didn't mind the mile-long walk to meet the school bus. He went on an old dirt road, one that was once used by loggers, his father told him, that wound through the woods and skirted the lake. It was a good road for Harold's game: he could spring out from behind huge oak trees to surprise passing villains and snatch their ill-gotten gains, and then disappear again into the forest. Before he reached the bus stop, though, he was tired of playing. The morning quiet in the woods got him to thinking about himself and to wish that his parents wouldn't worry about him so much. He didn't mind being alone, but he was ashamed to say so. He was ashamed to tell his parents that he had special friends that they didn't know about. He would rather die than tell his teacher or have any of the kids in school know that he had a secret, imaginary life.

When he thought about it, he was even ashamed of his secret life. People might think he was crazy. And when he put everything together: an absolute failure at making friends at school, not minding being alone, and having that private life that he kept to himself . . . well, he thought he probably was crazy.

Harold couldn't remember exactly how it had started or when. Probably the year before when one morning he had gotten up very early with his father. His father had to be on his route when it was just beginning to get light. After they had a hearty breakfast together, and Harold had waved his father off, he had wandered down to the lake, which was a short distance from his house.

Harold loved the lake but he had never been there so early in the morning. The sun was just rising over the hills on the opposite shore and light, fluffy, pink clouds floated by like mounds of cotton candy. Harold thought he had never seen anything so beautiful. The lake had been very still and quiet that summer morning. Standing alone in a cove, his bare feet touching the cool water, Harold had felt his skinny, four-foot-nine-inch body grow—as if suddenly he had blown up to be big and powerful.

Harold had sat down on a rock to think. Because he spent so much time alone,

Harold was a great reader. He especially loved adventure stories and books about people like Charles Lindbergh and Hank Aaron, and about men who climbed mountains and sailed in search of whales and went in spaceships to the moon. He loved heroes. As he sat on the rock, he thought that if only he could do something tremendous, he wouldn't be a disappointment to his parents, and all the kids in school would want him for a friend.

What if someone out in the lake were drowning, and he swam out and saved him? Or an escaped lion was in the woods and he caught it? Or an airplane had to make an emergency landing in the woods, and he pulled the passengers out of the burning wreckage?

Harold had let his imagination run wild, and he had lost himself completely in thinking of all the marvelous, heroic feats he could accomplish. He couldn't believe it when his mother called him and said it was

almost nine o'clock and she had to leave to go to work. He had sat there dreaming for almost three hours!

After that morning, Harold spent as much time at the lake as he could. Sometimes he brought a book along and read, but more often he thought about his secret life: the

life of a hero. He imagined going up to the moon; he imagined catching the biggest whale in the world; he thought about building an enormous bridge across the ocean, or flying around the world in a day. Perhaps he would hit a terrific home run the last inning of a baseball game and lead his team to victory. He saw himself carried around the field on the shoulders of the boys on his team. Once in a while he even thought about being elected President of the United States. Anything was possible when he sat at the lake by himself.

Harold's lake was special because it hadn't always been there. Harold could barely remember when it had been a river, before the electric company had built a huge dam ten miles downstream to get more power for the neighboring towns. About thirteen miles of the river had been dammed up and widened. Since the lake was only five years old, and was surrounded by steep cliffs, the area was not built up. Very few people had houses on the shore. Harold was glad that his parents had built their house before he was born and that now it was close to the new lake.

He felt as if the little patch of sand, the rocks, and that particular cove of the lake belonged to him exclusively, and when he was there he could be transformed into anyone he wanted to be. He also made friends at the lake. He got to know the birds. His parents had given him a guide to wild birds for a birthday present so that he could identify the different species. He learned to recognize the melancholy call of the mourning dove, the chattering of the chickadees, and to feel excitement at the beauty of the cardinals, the bluejays, and the redwing blackbirds. Often he brought a pocketful of bird seed with him and scattered it on the sand and the rocks. He liked to think that the birds knew him, too. The idea made him feel spe-

cial and not lonely. Sometimes he wrote
down lists of the birds he saw:

Canada goose	6
mourning dove	8
horned lark	12
common crow	9
junco	7
white-throated sparrow	6
white-breasted nuthatch	3
goldfinch	8

One day, about the middle of that summer, a new family had arrived in Harold's
cove: a mother duck and her five ducklings.
For Harold it had been love at first sight.
He had been so entranced watching the
mother duck and her babies glide in the
water, waddle up to the shore, ruffle their
feathers, dive back into the water, that he
hadn't thought about anything else that day.
The next morning he couldn't wait to get
down to the lake to see if the ducks were
still there. He brought a handful of grain

with him and threw it out for them to eat.

Every day that summer and late into the fall Harold went down to the lake to see the ducks and to feed them. He felt less alone than ever, and with the ducks as his audience, he could watch them, and still think his favorite thoughts. Many times Harold acted out the stories he made up. He'd run up and down the beach in pretend games. "Watch out, a plane's landing," he'd call out to an imaginary friend. "Get out of the way, QUICK." And he would drop flat on the ground, peering out of the tall grass for the plane. Or he would lead an underwater expedition. "Come on, get ready, we're going to dig for treasure at the bottom of the ocean. Put on your snorkels and oxygen tanks," he'd say. Sometimes he brought his toy gun to the beach and made believe he had a shoot-out with robbers. If the weather was warm Harold would dive into the water with the ducks. The ducks became part of the games he played. They were his friends.

But when winter came to the hills of New England, the lake froze over. With nowhere to swim, the ducks went away. Harold was very sad. He missed the ducks so much, and because the weather was very cold, he couldn't spend much time at the lake. But he still made up in his head a lot of stories about accomplishing great feats: sitting at his desk he might be a war hero and pretend he was riding through the streets in an open car with people cheering on all sides; or standing by the window he could be a fireman rescuing children from a burning house; or he could be a policeman grappling on the floor with a thief. But he liked playing at the lake best because there was more space and more to do, and he could shout out loud since there was no one but the ducks to hear him.

Harold was happy when the weather turned warm again and he could go back to the lake and play his games. But the ducks hadn't returned yet and without them, it

14

wasn't the same. He kept hoping that they would come back.

On that warm, sunny day early in June, when Harold came home from school, he grabbed the stick that was a spear and went down to the lake. And there were the ducks: a mother and five ducklings. Harold was sure they were the very same ducks from the previous summer, his friends. "Probably not," his father said when Harold came home, all excited. "The baby ducks would be grown up by now."

"Well, maybe the mother is one of them grown up, with her own babies," Harold said. "I'm sure they're the same family. I just know it."

His father laughed and said, "It's okay if you want to think that."

Harold was looking forward to the end of school when he could again go down to the

lake early in the morning. Everything would be the same as it had been the summer before—he could spend as much time at the lake as he wanted, his ducks were there, and he could play his favorite games.

But Harold soon discovered that everything was not the same. Someone had set up a marina a few miles below his cove, and now there were boats on the lake that had not been there before. Even early in the morning, men were out fishing from the boats. What was worse, they came and fished in his cove, and sometimes picnicked on the sand and left beer cans and garbage.

Harold didn't like it. He felt that his own private place had been invaded. And what was more annoying, he couldn't play his games freely the way he had before. As he reasoned with himself. "If anyone saw me running up and down the beach, shouting out orders with no one around, they'd surely think I was nuts." Those men fishing really got Harold mad.

And that wasn't the worst of it.

One day, when he came home from school, Harold was sitting on his favorite rock reliving one of his favorite stories. "Quick, quick," he called out to the ducks, "an emergency call on the lake. Boat capsized. . . ." He jumped up and was making believe he was getting into a boat, when he heard someone coming through the woods behind him. Harold swung around, sensing danger, and was rather disappointed to see a young woman in shorts walking toward him.

"Hi there," she said with a wide smile. "What lovely ducks."

"Yeah." Harold had never seen her before and didn't think she had any business walking onto his cove as if she owned it.

"You live around here?"

"Yeah. In the red house." It was the only house in sight. Where did she think he lived?

"Good. Then we're neighbors." She put out her hand. "I'm Cindy Adams. My husband and I just bought this property. We're living in our camper while we start building our house."

Harold touched her hand gingerly. He was too shocked to be cordial. "You bought this cove?" His voice squeaked.

"As much as we could. Up to the highwater mark. The power company owns the rest. And a couple of acres in the woods. It was more than we could afford but we fell in love with it. It's a beautiful spot."

"It sure is," Harold said glumly. He couldn't believe what he had just heard. He had never thought about anyone owning his beach. He felt betrayed. He didn't even want to look at the woman, although his first glance had told him she was good-looking enough with blue eyes and short, curly hair. As far as he was concerned, however, she could be an ugly monster.

"What's your name?" she asked in a friendly voice.

"Harold Coyle," he mumbled. "I guess I'd better be going."

"Don't go on my account. These ducks are adorable. They yours?"

"Not exactly. They're wild. But they live here. I feed them. But I guess I won't any more."

"Why not? Listen, Tom, my husband, and I don't mind if you come down to the cove. You like it here, don't you?"

"It's my favorite place in the whole world," Harold said forlornly.

The woman laughed. "Don't sound so sad about it. We don't want a bunch of strangers here, like whoever leaves garbage around," she said, picking up two beer cans from the sand, "but you can come as much and as often as you want. It was yours before it became ours," she added generously.

"You mean it?" Harold asked eagerly.

"Of course I mean it. You can be a big help to us too, if you don't mind. We're not going to have much time to spend down here this summer, we'll be too busy working on our house. But maybe you could keep an eye out, and tell strangers to keep off. Tell them it's private property. We don't want any garbage dumped here."

"I'll do that. I sure will." Harold felt relieved, although he still had a sad feeling that his beach would never be the same again. It would never be his own private place.

But after he had helped her clean up the litter and she had brought a big plastic bag from her camper to dump the cans and garbage into, some of Harold's proprietary feelings came back. Somebody else must have owned that piece of beach before, he figured, so it really didn't make too much difference now. He was still going to think of it as his.

When Harold went home he told his mother about their new neighbors. "Too bad it's not a family with children," she said. "Then you'd have playmates nearby."

"Mmmm," was all Harold said. He could tell by his mother's face that she was worrying again about his not having any friends. Harold wished he wasn't such a disappointment. But he didn't like playing baseball or football or hockey, or any of the things the other kids did. He liked to watch birds, and he loved his ducks, and he liked to be by himself to think a lot of things. He couldn't help it if he was peculiar.

Harold was glad there were only a few days of school left. He wanted to be down at the lake to carry out his job for the Adamses, to keep trespassers off their beach. At school everyone was talking about the class picnic for the last day.

"Where do you want to go?" Mrs. Evans, the teacher, asked Harold's class.

"Some place where we can go swimming," Frank Rugby said.

"It's too cold in Connecticut to swim in early June," Mrs. Evans said.

"Let's not have a picnic, let's go to New York," Betty Crane suggested.

"And sit under a tree in Central Park to eat our sandwiches," said Dizzy Jacobs, laughing heartily at his own joke.

"I think we should go to the state park," Dick Alden said. "Everything's there. Tennis courts and volleyball, and if Frank wants to swim there's a place in the river. They have picnic tables and fireplaces for cooking. It's great."

Everyone applauded that idea. Everyone except Harold. He had different ideas for a picnic. To him a picnic should be an excursion into the unknown, a place you had never been to before. He thought of following a stream to see where it came from and where it went. Or climbing a mountain just to get to the top. Or discovering some small piece of wilderness, a wildlife refuge in the marshes perhaps, or going down into an old cave to look for minerals. . . .

"What's so great about the state park?" Harold asked. "We've all been there a million times."

"You never like to do anything that everyone else does," the girl sitting next to him commented.

"That's because he can't do them," Frank Rugby said. "All he likes to do is watch birds. Harold, the nutty bird watcher."

Harold flushed and wished for the hundredth time that he had never brought in his list of birds for a nature-study assignment. His teacher had been impressed and had insisted that he tell about his bird watching, but the children had teased him ever since. Someday he'd show them. Someday he'd do something that would make them all sorry they had ever made fun of him. Someday he'd show the whole school, his parents, and the whole town that Harold Coyle wasn't a peculiar drip.

The day of the class picnic Harold lay on a long, flat rock jutting out into the river, thinking maybe this would be the day. Maybe something terrific would happen and he'd show them he was no little runt, he'd do something that would make them all sit up and take notice. He'd be a hero and everyone would applaud him. He'd have a million friends. His mind roamed from one possibility to another: maybe Mrs. Evans would have a heart attack and he'd give her mouth-to-mouth resuscitation and save her life; or maybe a monster would come out of the woods and he'd pick up a stick and knock it over the head; or maybe a kidnapper would come along to steal one of the girls, and he would catch him.

"Harold, the boys are playing ball. Why don't you go and join them?" Mrs. Evans was standing on the slope above him.

"I don't feel like it," Harold told her.

"I don't think you should just lie here all day. Get up and do something."

Harold wished she would leave him alone, but he pulled himself up. "All right, all right," he muttered.

He certainly wasn't going to play ball. Harold surveyed the scene. The best thing about the state park as far as he was concerned were the cliffs and rocks that bordered the river. He now started to climb them, going upstream. He clambered up and down the rocks with his goal High Rock, a huge hunk of stone that jutted some fifteen feet over the river. It was a favorite jumping-off place for swimmers in the summertime.

Harold was agile and it didn't take him long to reach the big rock. He felt good standing there alone, higher than anyone around him, looking out over the river. He could hear the children below clustered around the soda stand opposite High Rock. As usual, Harold's thoughts took flight. This rock, he thought, must have been around since the beginning of time. Maybe Colonial militiamen had fought here against the British soldiers. Or Indians had shot their arrows to kill a deer from this vantage point, or perhaps defended themselves against a band of white men come to steal their land. Harold felt himself a brave Indian chief. He straightened up his small body and made believe he had a bow and arrow in his hands. With an erect back and narrowed eyes he held his imaginary bow with his left arm outstretched, and his right hand hold-

ing the arrow in place. With his eyes fixed on the target of a white birch across the narrow river channel, Harold took sight along the length of his imaginary arrow and inched forward, his only thought to get in the best position to hit his enemy. Suddenly there was nothing but empty space beneath his left foot, and Harold went over the edge and hurtled down to the water below.

The river was still very high from the spring rains, and in a second Harold was struggling in the strong currents. He was not a good swimmer although he knew how to stay above water, and the weight of his wet jeans and sweater and his sneakers pulled him down. He tried to scramble up on a rock but he kept slipping back. There was nothing to grab hold of.

"Help," he screamed at the top of his voice. "Help, help." He panicked and went under, thinking that no one could possibly hear him. He came up with a mouthful of water and was terrified. He could hear the children's voices, and tried to scream again. "Help, help. . . ."

He tried desperately to get some leverage on a rock and felt himself slipping again. It was horrible to be so close to shore and to be drowning . . . he was slipping beneath the water when there was a splash and an arm encircled him, pulling him up onto the rocks.

Someone was bending over him, thumping on his back, and he was bringing up a gush of water. He knew there was a circle of people around him although everything looked blurry. Then he upchucked.

Minutes later Harold was sitting up in his dripping clothes with Mrs. Evans and Frank Rugby beside him.

"Are you all right now?" Mrs. Evans was looking at him with worried eyes. "Frank here saved your life."

"He did?" Harold didn't know what to say. He couldn't believe what had happened. He knew he ought to thank Frank; he knew he ought to do something big and important to show how grateful he was, but all he felt was horribly, terribly ashamed.

"Boy, you really came close," Frank said, his eyes bright with excitement, his own clothes as wet as Harold's. "It's a good thing I heard you or you would have had it. How in the world did you do that, anyway?"

"I don't know. I was just standing there, and then I was falling down. . . ." He wasn't going to tell them he was making believe he was an Indian chief. "You were great, Frank. Terrific, honest. I kept trying to grab hold of a rock, but they were all so slippery. I'm sorry, honest. . . ."

"Forget it," Frank said. "I said I wanted to go swimming, didn't I?"

"You boys better get in the sun and dry out," Mrs. Evans said. "You can take your wet shirts off, and your sneakers too, Harold. Frank had the sense to kick his off before he went in."

Frank was the hero of the day. The children couldn't stop talking about the way he had jumped in and pulled Harold out. "You ought to be a lifesaver," they said to Frank.

"I am a junior lifesaver," Frank admitted proudly.

"I bet you were real scared," one of the boys said to Harold. "You would have drowned if it hadn't been for Frank."

"Yes, I know," Harold said morosely. He almost wished he had drowned. He had never felt so terrible in his whole life. He felt ashamed and angry. He didn't know what he was angry at. Maybe angry that he wasn't big and strong like Frank, angry that he had done anything so dumb as fall into the river. He felt like a stupid fool because he knew, even if no one else did, that he dreamed all the time that he was the one to save people. No one knew how much he thought about being a hero. . . . And here he was, the dumb jerk who had to be fished out of the river by Frank. Harold felt as if life had betrayed him—as if someone had played a mean trick on him.

Harold was very glad that the picnic was the last day of school. Maybe by September everyone would forget that he was the dope who had to be saved from drowning. By the time he came home his clothes were dry so he didn't have to tell his mother what had happened. That was some relief.

The first day of vacation, Saturday, Harold was happy to go down to his cove. It had rained during the night and the air felt as if it had been washed clean and sparkling like his mother's laundry. He had a marvelous sense of freedom. With no school, he could stay at the lake all day if he felt like it.

Harold sat on his favorite rock, for a change not thinking of anything in particular. A flock of catbirds were flying around but he wished they'd leave because they would frighten the other birds away. Harold had given up keeping a list of the birds he saw—that had been his bird phase, as his mother said—but he still liked to watch them. Now the ducks were his favorites. He didn't think he'd ever get tired of watching them.

Harold noticed there was more litter on the beach than before, but he felt lazy about cleaning it up. He had brought a garbage bag with him and he'd do it after a while. . . . In the meantime he stretched out on a patch of sand between the rocks and gazed up at the sky. But Harold never stayed still for long and in a short while he was on his feet, making believe he was picking up treasures that had been washed ashore as he gathered up the beer cans and crumpled food wrappings from the ground. "Aha . . . a thousand pounds of gold," he called out to the ducks, spearing some papers with a stick. "A casket of diamonds and rubies," he cried as he picked up a beer can filled with sand.

He stopped short, embarrassed, as a small boat came into the cove with its outboard motor off. "Hey, son," the man in the boat called. "I've got something for you." He took a bag from amidst the fishing gear, rope, rubber boots, pail, and miscellaneous items strewn around the bottom of the boat and flung it to Harold on the shore. "You can add this to what you've got."

The bag landed at Harold's feet and split open, spilling a pile of unappetizing garbage on his sneakers.

"Hey, this isn't a garbage dump," Harold yelled. "Look what you did . . . You can't throw your junk here. . . ."

The man laughed. "Didn't mean for it to break. Sorry." He turned the boat around, pulled on the motor, and took off.

Harold stared after him, furious. "I'll get him," he muttered. "I'll cut him up into little pieces and feed him to the fishes." Harold wished he was big and strong and could really beat that guy up.

A few days later Harold was at the lake when a young man came along he figured must be Mr. Adams. It was. The man introduced himself as Tom.

"It's a beautiful lake," Tom said, looking out over the water. "I sure hope it doesn't get ruined. You spend a lot of time down here?" he asked Harold.

"Yeah. Mrs. Adams said she didn't mind. I've been coming down here for a long time."

"That's all right. I don't mind . . . it's

only. . . ." Harold could feel Tom looking at him, and he saw an expression on his face something like the one he often saw in his mother's eyes: What's the matter with you, why do you hang around here, why don't you have any friends? Why aren't you playing with other kids? It made Harold feel funny and he got up to go.

"Say," Tom said, "if you haven't anything else to do, maybe you'd like to help me? I'm going to be doing some clearing, for our house, you know. I'll be sawing down some big trees, but maybe you could help me with the small stuff. Gather up the twigs and brush. Would you like that? I'd pay you. How much do you get?"

"I dunno. Sometimes my father gives me fifty cents an hour for stacking wood. I've never worked for anyone else."

"Fifty cents an hour's fine with me. Okay?"

"That'd be great." Harold was excited. "When do you want me to start?"

"We can start right now. You want to go home and tell your mother where you are?"

"My mother's working. She's not home."

"Okay, then, let's go."

Harold followed Tom back through the woods to the van. He had never been inside a camper before, and he was delighted to be invited in for a soda. "Boy, this is neat," Harold said. The camper had everything: There was a couch and chairs and a table for eating. Cindy explained that the couch opened up into a bed. There was even a small refrigerator and stove. Harold thought it was wonderful.

After Cindy and Tom had coffee and Harold had his soda, they went to work. Cindy and Harold gathered up fallen twigs while Tom cut down small brush. Then Tom got out his big power saw and said he was going to cut down a tall ash tree. It was exciting to watch the saw, held firmly in Tom's strong hands, cut through the big tree. "Out of the way," Tom called out. He knew exactly where the tree was going to fall. Cindy and Harold stood by to watch the tree come crashing down in the very place Tom said it would.

They worked steadily all morning. Tom cut down two more big trees. When Harold went home for the lunch his mother had set out for him, he had two and a half dollars for five hours of work. He felt like a millionaire.

Working with Tom gave Harold a lot of new things to think about. When he went back to the lake after lunch he sat on his favorite rock and thought about Tom. Cindy said that Tom could do anything: he was going to dig a foundation for their house and run all the wires for electricity and put in pipes for plumbing. He could do stonework and carpentry. Harold began to imagine that he was someone like Tom. He could be a lumberman working in the forests clearing out lumber for the mills. Or he could build the finest houses in the world, houses that people from all over would come to admire.

He could go to India and build houses for poor people. He would be big and strong and have great bulging muscles in his arms and legs the way Tom had. A real, live hero had come into Harold's life, someone he truly admired and wanted to copy.

Harold was so busy with his fantasies he didn't notice the fishing boat that was nearing the shore until he heard a man calling him. Harold recognized the man as the same one who had thrown the bag of garbage to him. "Hey, these ducks yours?" the man called out.

Harold hesitated for a few seconds. He suddenly felt threatened. He didn't like the way the man was looking at the ducks. But he wasn't good at telling outright lies. "Not really," he said. "They're mine in a way—I feed them."

"I didn't think they belonged to anyone. They're wild. Nice-looking ducks. . . ."

"They live here," Harold said.

"That's what I thought." The man kept

looking at the ducks in a way that Harold liked less and less. The man was burly with greedy eyes and he looked as if he might gobble those ducks up right then and there.

The man cut off his motor and headed his boat into the shore. In a few minutes he got out of the boat and, wading in the water, pulled the boat up on the beach.

"Nice spot here," he said. Harold watched him take a lunch box out of the boat and sit down on a rock to eat. Harold didn't know what to do. He felt he was failing Cindy and Tom, but he didn't feel like much of a hero; he was scared of the man. Finally he said, "This is private property. They don't want any strangers here."

The man let out a loud laugh. "Is that so? So I'm not a stranger. You can call me Spike. Pleased to meet you. What's your name?"

"My name's Harold." He didn't want this man for a friend. He screwed up his courage to talk to Spike. "I guess it's all right this

time, but I'm supposed to keep people off here. I work for the people who own it."

This time the man laughed even louder. "You're supposed to keep people off. That's a good one . . . you'd better grow up some before you take on a job like that. I like it here. The fishing's good in this cove—I get some of my best fish here. You better tell your friends I ain't gonna stop coming here."

He ate up his sandwiches, drank his beer, and got up. "It's real pretty here. . . ." He peeled a banana and dropped the peel in the sand along with his empty beer can and wrappings.

"Don't leave your garbage here," Harold said. "You take that with you."

The man stared at him. "Who's gonna make me?"

Harold had no answer. He felt choked up with anger. "I'm going to tell the owners . . . I'll tell them who did this."

"You do that, sonny. You tell them Spike

was here and left his calling card." The man let out a loud laugh and pushed off in his boat.

Harold ran up to the camper and told Cindy and Tom. He was almost in tears. "I didn't know how to stop him," he said.

"Don't try," Tom said. "A guy like that is just mean. Some people are born that way, or life makes them that way. He's the kind that steals candy from babies. Not that you're a baby, Harold," Tom added quickly. "You did the right thing. Don't tangle with a stupid bully like that."

But after that day, Spike was all that Harold could think about. He imagined himself beating Spike to a pulp, or standing by smiling while Spike was in the water drowning and begging for help and Harold saving him only at the last minute; he saw himself driving a fantastic sports car and passing Spike hobbling along the road begging for a lift and Harold stopping only long enough to hand him a bag of garbage. . . .

45

Harold's mind spun endless fantasies of himself and the burly man with the small, beady eyes.

But reality was very different from Harold's dreams. He came down to the lake every day to see his ducks and to feed them, but his private place was no longer the same. Because of the new marina there were lots of boats and many of them came into his cove. The boats and fishermen discouraged the birds so there were not as many to watch. His sense of privacy was now almost all gone. How could he play his games when a boat could drop anchor in his cove any time? He felt more and more frustrated about Spike. Tom no longer had any work for him to do and Harold felt unhappy and angry with himself that the one job he could do for his friends, to keep an undesirable stranger off their beach, was the one thing he could not do.

Spike didn't come every day, but he came often enough. A few times Harold ran up to get Tom when he saw Spike's boat coming, but either Tom wasn't there, or if he did come down to the lake Spike had disappeared. "Forget about it," Tom said to Harold. "One of these days I'll get him, but in the meantime I don't want you to hassle with him."

But actually that was exactly what Harold did want. Although he was afraid of Spike, Spike was the *Bad Man*, and Harold wanted to be the Hero, the *Good Guy* who got rid of him. Sometimes he talked about his feelings to the ducks. In a way they were his best friends. They were so independent, living their lives in the water, calmly swimming about, waddling on to the shore. They never seemed disturbed. Harold loved to watch them and he also felt protective of them. He felt as if they belonged to him.

"Of course he's bigger than I am," he said to the ducks, speaking of Spike, "but I think I'm smarter. He doesn't even know how to run his boat that good. Sometimes he can't get the motor started, he doesn't let it cool off, just keeps trying to start it up over and over again using terrible language. He's a stupid jerk."

"I don't know what you do with yourself all day down at the lake," Harold's mother said to him one morning before she left for work. There were days when she left early in the morning and didn't come home until six or seven in the evening. "I do worry about you being alone so much."

"I have Tom and Cindy," Harold said. And I have the ducks, he thought to himself, and Spike, although of course Spike wasn't a friend; but he was a presence in Harold's life. The only days he really felt lonesome were when it rained and he had to stay in the house.

"The Adamses are grown-ups. They aren't children for you to play with," his mother said with that familiar, worried look in her eyes.

Harold again felt his failure: he was no

good to anyone, a disappointment and worry to his parents and not even able to protect the beach for Cindy and Tom. He felt all he was good for was to clean up the garbage stupid Spike left behind.

And so the summer days went by, one day like another. Harold didn't see Spike very often. He came either very early in the morning before Harold got down to the water, or in the dusk when Harold had gone home. But Harold knew Spike had come by the familiar small pile of garbage he left.

One morning there was more than garbage to show Spike had been around. His little pile of garbage was there all right, but there was also the remains of a fire he had built on the sand, undoubtedly the evening before.

Harold eyed the ashes suspiciously and let out a cry when he saw some feathers and small bones. With a dreadful premonition he ran to the water's edge to look for the ducks. There was the mother duck lead-

ing her young ones, and Harold counted:
one, two, three, four. . . . Harold looked
all around, perhaps the fifth one had gone
off by himself, perhaps. . . . Harold sat
with his eyes glued to the water, hoping as
hard as he had ever hoped for anything in
his life that the fifth duck would appear. But
it didn't. Harold counted again: one, two,
three, four.

He avoided looking at the remains of the fire when he turned back to the beach. He felt too sad even to cry. Then he made himself go to the pile and solemnly he scooped up the tiny bones and the few feathers and buried them in the woods at the edge of the beach. He felt totally alone. He couldn't stay at the beach. He didn't want to see Spike if he came back today.

With slow steps Harold walked up the path to where Cindy and Tom's camper stood in a clearing in the woods. Not far away they were both working on the foundation for their new house.

Cindy looked up and greeted Harold. "What's the matter? Has that man been bothering you again?"

Harold had to swallow a few times before he could speak. "He killed one of the ducks," he said flatly.

Tom stopped working. "Are you sure? How do you know?"

"I know." Harold told them about the fire and Spike's familiar empty beer can and sandwich wrappings, and the remains of the duck. "And one's gone. He did it."

"That's the worst thing I ever heard," Cindy said. "What can we do?" She turned to her husband.

Tom shook his head sadly. "I don't know. Not much, I'm afraid. We'd have to catch him and even then it wouldn't be easy to hold him until we got the police. I can't stay down there twenty-four hours a day waiting for him. It's a lousy situation."

"But we've got to do something," Cindy insisted. "He might. . . ." She glanced at Harold and stopped short.

Harold nodded his head forlornly. "Yeah. He might kill all the ducks."

"I can call the police and tell them, and call the marina. But I know what the cops will say. They'll say they can't do anything unless they actually catch him breaking the law—trespassing or hunting without a license." Tom looked from Cindy to Harold. "I know it's terrible, but that's the way it is."

"I don't think you should stay down there alone so much," Cindy said to Harold. "That man is vicious and there's no telling what he might do."

"I'll be okay," Harold said gruffly. He knew he had no intention of staying away from the beach and he wasn't going to make any such promise to Cindy.

But when he left Cindy and Tom he did

not go back to the beach. Harold walked through the woods thinking. Maybe Tom believed there was nothing to be done, but Harold thought otherwise. He was determined to do something. But what? He thought and thought until he had a headache. By the time he came home he had a half-formed plan in his mind.

Harold spent the remainder of the day restlessly. He didn't feel like reading, he didn't want to watch television, he didn't know what he wanted to do. He didn't want to go down to the lake—not yet. That day Harold felt his aloneness as a big burden. He thought it would be nice to have a friend, to have someone he could talk to; they could plan together what to do about that vicious man, Spike. Harold felt that the private world he had lived in had been blown to bits—just as if the enemy had bombed it, and he would never have it to live in any more. It was a funny feeling—like stepping out of a familiar room into an unknown corridor and not knowing which way to go. He was both afraid and excited.

That evening, around dusk, Harold decided to try his plan. It wasn't an exact plan, and Harold wasn't at all sure how it would work, but he knew that he had to take some action. His mother wasn't home yet, and his father was watching the news on television. Harold told his father he was going outside for a bit.

He walked down the path to the lake, and as he came close to the edge of the woods, he crept stealthily, not wanting to make a sound. This was the time of day, Harold figured, when it was almost dark, that Spike would come to catch another dinner for himself.

He waited and waited but there was no sign of the burly man. Harold felt cramped lying on the ground, but he waited until it was really dark and he could see the first evening star. Disappointed, he got up and went home.

"Where have you been so late?" his mother scolded him. "We've been waiting for you to eat."

"I was just outside," Harold said.

The next morning he ran down to the lake early. He was worried that maybe Spike had come after dark, when he had left. And sure enough the signs of the previous evening's meal were there. Not even wanting to look, Harold counted the ducks. There was the mother, and one, two, three young ducklings following her. Harold counted twice, to be sure. This time he could not hold back his tears. He sat down on his rock and sobbed.

Harold didn't want to go up to see Cindy and Tom. He knew that they couldn't do anything. If anyone was going to catch Spike, it was going to have to be him.

Harold hung around the lake most of the day, but he was sure that Spike wasn't going to appear until dark. That night he was determined to keep watch. After supper he told his mother he was going outside to catch fireflies. "Don't stay out too long," his mother said.

Once again Harold walked down the path through the woods, and crept stealthily as he neared the lake. He knew his way perfectly in the dark. He didn't have to use the flashlight he had stuck in his pocket. He lay flat on his stomach at the edge of the woods, with his eyes glued on the lake. Harold didn't know how long he lay there, his body getting chilly and cramped. It could have been ten minutes or half an hour—it seemed like a long time to him.

Then, he heard the sound of a motor on the water. His heart started to beat rapidly. Harold lifted up his head, and sure enough a familiar boat was heading in to the shore. Harold heard the motor cut off, and from his hidden spot he watched Spike pull his boat onto the sand. He watched the man gather kindling for a fire, and take out a blanket and his lunch box from the boat. He was getting ready for another feast.

Spike let out a call that sent the shivers up Harold's spine, but brought out the ducks. Harold watched the man pick up a shotgun, and stand to aim. In a flash Harold sprang from his hiding place and made a diving tackle for Spike's legs. Taken by complete surprise, and standing on uneven ground, the heavy man toppled over and dropped his gun in the sand. Harold grabbed the gun and ran.

He ran faster than he'd ever run in his life, through the woods where there was hardly a path, straight for the camper. Spike was running after him, yelling, "Stop, thief, hey you, give me back my gun!"

Harold knew the woods and Spike did not, and he could hear the man stumbling in the dark. Harold was gasping for breath when he reached the camper.

"What happened? What's going on?" Cindy and Tom brought Harold inside. "Are you all right?"

Harold handed the gun to Tom. "Here, take this. It's Spike's. I caught him—he was about to shoot another duck." Rapidly he told the astonished couple what had happened.

"It's fantastic," Cindy kept repeating.

They could all hear Spike coming up toward the camper, still yelling to get his gun back. Tom stood at the door of the camper with the gun in his hand. "I'm going to hold him here," he said to Harold. "You go out the back way and run to your house and call the police. We'll get him this time," he said with grim satisfaction.

Harold had barely caught his breath when he was off again. He raced back to his house

60

and he tried to explain to his parents and call the state police all at once. After he got the police barracks, he told his mother and father a little more quietly about the terrible man and the ducks. "Good heavens," his mother cried, hugging him, "you could have gotten shot."

"I didn't," Harold said.

"You did a terrific job," his father said proudly.

His father went back with him to the camper and in a short while a police car drove up and two officers got out. Spike, who had been sitting outside the camper with Tom pointing the gun at him, started to talk immediately. "That young squirt was stealing my gun . . . he was running away with it."

"That's not true," Harold cried. "He was about to shoot another duck."

Between the two of them, Tom and Harold explained to the policemen.

"Let's see your hunting license," one of

the troopers said, walking up to Spike.

Spike made as if to search through his pockets and then admitted he didn't have one.

"I'd like to take a look at your boat," the policeman said. "We're looking for a stolen boat."

Harold led the trooper down to the shore and the policeman examined the boat with his flashlight. "This seems to be the one we're looking for. I guess we'd better take that character to the station house."

When they got back to the camper the officer asked Tom to tell him again exactly what had happened. Tom told him about the trespassing and the duck shooting. "Two ducks," Harold commented, and Harold finished the story with what had happened that night.

Both the officers looked at Harold in wonder. "You mean you tackled this man? By yourself, and he had a gun?" one of them asked.

Harold nodded. "Yeah. I didn't really think about it. I just did it. I was real mad at him for killing those ducks."

"I guess you were," the officer laughed. "You're a terrific kid. You did a great job tonight. You may have caught someone we've been trying to get hold of for months—I have a hunch we'll find this subject has a history of break-ins, poaching, and thievery. I think you may have caught a real dangerous criminal."

Harold opened his eyes wide. "You mean it?"

"You're a hero," Tom said.

"I'll say you are," his father agreed.

Harold had a hard time falling asleep that night. He couldn't believe what had happened. After all his dreaming, all his fantasizing, could it be possible that he truly was a hero? He didn't feel much like a hero—although he didn't know what a hero felt like. But he didn't feel any different from before. Except his body was stiff from lying cramped on the ground. And he was glad, very glad that he had saved another duck from getting killed.

The next morning Harold got up as usual and went down to the lake. He watched the birds and he watched the ducks and he was happy that the burly man was no longer going to come and leave garbage or shoot a duck. He was still at the lake when Cindy came running down. "Harold, you did it, you did it!"

She was almost too excited to talk. "That man was the man the cops were looking for. He has a jail record. You caught a real thief!"

Harold was astounded. "You mean it? How about that . . . I guess it's a good thing I didn't know or I would have been too scared to do anything."

"You're a very brave boy to do what you did," Cindy said. "A newspaper reporter is here. He got the story from the police and he wants to interview you. Come on back to the camper, he's waiting for you."

Now Harold really got nervous. "I don't want to talk to a reporter. I won't know what to say."

"Don't worry, he'll ask all the questions."

And that's what the reporter did. He had a notebook and he asked Harold all about his school, what sports he went in for, what his hobbies were.

Harold felt embarrassed. "I don't much like sports, and I don't have exactly what you'd call hobbies. I spend a lot of time at the lake."

"Then you must swim a lot."

"I do sometimes."

"What do you do?"

"Nothing much," Harold said. He couldn't tell anyone that he made up games for himself down at the lake. Harold could tell that the reporter was pretty disappointed in him, even though he took his picture. Maybe being a one-time hero wasn't any big deal. He was still a disappointment to everyone.

Yet when his father brought home the local newspaper the next day and they all saw Harold's picture on the front page and a big headline that said NINE-YEAR-OLD CATCHES THIEF, Harold felt pretty good. "We certainly are proud of you," his father said.

When a lot of his classmates from school called up to congratulate him his mother was especially pleased. "Now maybe you won't stay alone so much. You're famous."

But Harold kept hoping that something would happen to make him feel different. But it didn't. He still didn't want to join the Little League, he didn't want to go visit with a bunch of kids—he still preferred to stay down at the lake and watch the birds and the ducks and think his thoughts. Especially now that he had so much more to think about. He had conquered a real person, and he made up endless games that had him catching Spike at other villainous deeds.

But the truth was, he could tell, he was still a disappointment to his parents. Frank Rugby was the one who kept calling up the most, and finally Harold's mother persuaded him to ask Frank over. "He's such an outgoing, athletic boy, it will be good for you to have him for a friend."

Harold didn't look forward to having Frank over. He kept thinking of the time Frank had pulled him out of the river, and what a jerk he had felt. But Frank came over, and immediately asked to go down to the lake to see where Harold had captured the thief.

"It wasn't anything much," Harold said. "He fell over so easy."

"Show me where," Frank said.

Frank followed Harold down to the lake, and Harold showed him where he had been hiding and where Spike had pulled up his boat and had stood with his gun.

"I'll pretend I'm Spike and you come tackle me," Frank said.

"I'll have to knock you down."

"I don't care."

Harold was uneasy. He had never played pretend with anyone else before. But he stretched out on the ground, and he watched Frank make believe he was pulling a boat up to the shore, building a fire, and then taking up his gun. As soon as Frank pointed a stick to use as the gun at the ducks, Harold dashed out and grabbed his legs, and Frank fell over. Harold picked up the stick and pointed it at Frank. He was carried away by the game and instead of running to the woods he cried, "Hands up."

Frank obeyed, and Harold marched him to a tree and made believe he tied him to it.

As soon as they finished that game, Frank suggested another. "I'll be a cop this time, and you be a thief. You're going to break into that house over there," Frank said, pointing to a big tree. "I'll catch you in the act."

The two boys played one make-believe

game after another, taking turns being the hero and the villain. By the end of the afternoon, Harold's head was in a whirl. He'd had the best time he'd ever had, but it was hard to believe that big Frank Rugby liked to make believe the same way that he did.

It was late in the afternoon when the boys went back to Harold's house and sat down in the kitchen to have a soda.

"You like to play those games?" Harold ventured.

Frank nodded. "Yeah, sure. It's more fun when you play with someone. I had a good time. Didn't you?"

"Yeah," Harold agreed.

When Frank left to go home, Harold sat and thought for a long while. This day he hadn't done anything so unusual. He had made up things the way he always had, but *now* he *felt* different. He hadn't been a hero this day, but he had made a big discovery. Maybe he wasn't just a shrimpy kook. Maybe there were lots of kids who liked to play make-believe, who made up great stories about themselves that never really happened.

Even though he had been a real hero once, Harold didn't think that made much difference. He couldn't help it if his parents were disappointed in him—there was a lot they didn't know about him. But that was okay because he knew, and he didn't feel peculiar anymore. Harold had to laugh at the way he and Frank had played together. If anyone had heard them they would have thought both boys were crazy. But Harold didn't care. He was glad Frank had said he was coming back the next day. Harold felt good that night. He went outside to catch fireflies and made believe he was guarding a jarful of nuclear atoms that could blow up the world. He and Frank could use it tomorrow to play a new game.

ABOUT THE AUTHOR

Hila Colman has written many books for young people, a number of which have also been published in Spanish and other languages. Her *The Girl from Puerto Rico* won a special award from the Child Study Association. The author's great concern with the problems faced by contemporary youngsters is reflected in her stories. She enjoys traveling and calls Bridgewater, Connecticut, home.

ABOUT THE ILLUSTRATOR

Charles Robinson was a successful lawyer for ten years before he decided to make his weekend hobby his weekday profession as well. Since then, he has illustrated more than fifty books and has been the recipient of many awards and honors, including the Gold Medal of the Society of Illustrators in 1970. Mr. Robinson lives in New Jersey with his wife and three children.